OUTSIDE AND INSIDE BIRDS

BY SANDRA MARKLE

Aladdin Paperbacks
New York London Toronto Sydney Singapore

*The author would like to express special thanks to Dr. Kevin McGowan,
Associate Curator of Birds and Mammals at Cornell University, and
Georgann Schmalz, Ornithologist, Fernbank Science Center, for sharing
both their expertise and enthusiasm.*

First Aladdin Paperbacks edition June 2002
Copyright © 1994 by Sandra Markle

ALADDIN PAPERBACKS
An imprint of Simon & Schuster
Children's Publishing Division
1230 Avenue of the Americas
New York, NY 10020

The Library of Congress has cataloged the hardcover edition as follows:
Markle, Sandra.
Outside and inside birds / by Sandra Markle.—1st ed.
p.   cm.
Includes index.
ISBN 0-02-762312-2 (hc.)
1. Birds—Juvenile literature.   [1. Birds.]   I. Title.
QL676.2.M36   1994
598—dc20 93-38910
ISBN 0-689-85086-7 (Aladdin pbk.)

READER'S NOTE: *To help readers pronounce words that
may not be familiar to them, there is a pronunciation
guide on page 36. These words are italicized the first
time they appear in the text.*

*For my parents,
Robert and Dorothy Haldeman,
with love*

Look at all the snow geese, climbing higher and higher into the air. Do you ever wonder why most birds can fly and you can't? This book will let you take a close look at birds—outside and inside—and find out.

This young parrot is just getting its green adult feathers. Like hairs, feathers grow from special spots in the skin. Tightly curled, they grow inside a cone-shaped covering. When the feather is fully developed, this covering splits, the feather uncurls, and the covering falls off.

Wing and tail feathers, like this one, have a stiff shaft down the middle to make them strong.

One thing a bird has that you don't is feathers. In fact, no other living thing has feathers. Even birds that don't fly, like penguins and ostriches, have them. But feathers are especially important to birds that do fly.

Fluffy down, like the baby parrot's white feathers, keeps the bird warm without adding much weight. A bird has to be lightweight to fly. In an adult bird, down is like underwear. It is tucked under a coat of *contour* feathers, like the parrot's new green ones. Contour feathers make the bird's body smooth, so it can easily slip through the air when it flies.

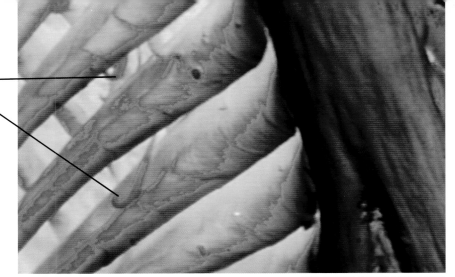

HOOKS

This picture is a very close look (enlarged 500 times) at one spot on an evening grosbeak's feather. You may be surprised to learn that feathers are made up of the same material as your fingernails.

COMPUTER COLOR-ENHANCED

Now, look at this close-up picture of a contour feather. Do you see the little hooks that hold the feather's branches together? When "zipped up," the feather forms a nearly airtight surface. Extra hooks at the edges of wing feathers catch onto the feathers next to them. This makes the whole wing airtight—just right for pushing against air to fly.

Wind, or brushing against something, can "unzip" feathers. Feathers also get dirty, and dirt adds weight. So birds spend a lot of time taking care of their feathers. This job is called preening. Some birds, like the great blue heron, have a special claw on their feet to comb their feathers. But most birds preen by pulling their feathers, one at a time, through their beaks.

Besides cleaning and combing, many birds also coat their feathers with oil. This oil comes from the preen gland. No one knows for sure exactly what this oil does. It seems to help make the feathers waterproof and to keep them from breaking.

Even well-cared-for feathers wear out, though. Then they have to be replaced with new ones. Because they need their wing feathers to fly, some birds, like golden eagles, replace feathers a few at a time on each wing. Others, like geese, lose all their flight feathers at once. Then they hide until their new feathers are fully grown.

Do you see the yellow spot on this brown pelican's tail? That is called the preen gland. When the bird squeezes the preen gland with its beak, oil comes out. Then the pelican rubs its oily beak over its feathers.

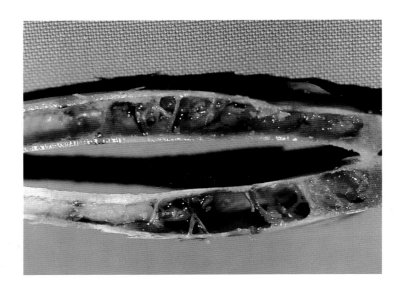

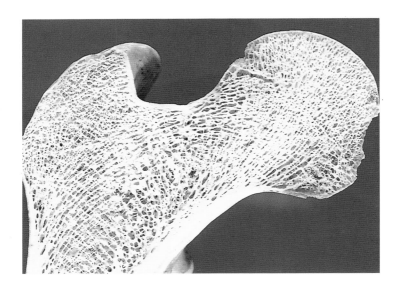

Many of a bird's bones are almost empty. In a living bird, this space would be filled with a balloon-like, air-filled sac.

Inside, your bone looks like a sponge with lots of spaces between hard bone.

Wonder what's under all those feathers? Bones, for one thing. A building has a strong framework to support it and give it shape. A bird's body, like your body, has a framework, too—a bony *skeleton*. Bones are hard, but they are not solid like rock. A bird's bones are even less solid than yours. In fact, some of a bird's bones are nearly hollow.

8

To make its skeleton even lighter, a bird does not have heavy jaw bones. In place of teeth, birds have bills. Gizzards, inside their bodies, help break down food, too.

Birds are also light because they have fewer joints. A joint is where two bones come together, like your knee and your elbow. Since a bird has fewer joints, it has fewer *muscles*, which are needed to move the bones—that means less weight.

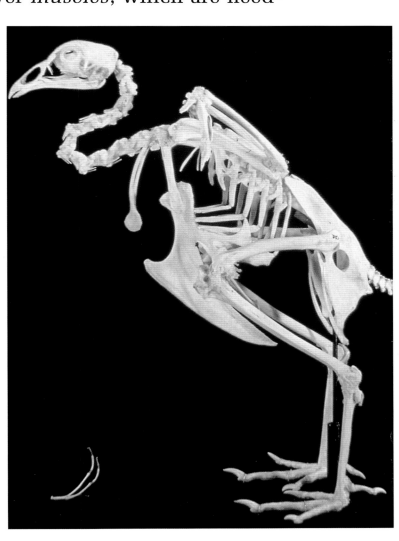

One part of a bird's body that has lots of joints is its neck. Birds use their beaks the way you use your fingers, so they need to be able to stretch and bend their necks freely. To make this possible, birds may have 15 neck bones; long-necked birds may have as many as 23. People and even giraffes only have 7 neck bones.

Next time you see an airplane, notice how its wings copy the shape of a bird's wing.

Look at the shape of the cliff swallow's wing—more curved above than on the bottom. Having wings shaped like this helps birds fly. To understand how this is possible, try this. Cut a strip of newspaper about five centimeters (two inches) wide and fifteen centimeters (six inches) long. Holding the long edges, put one short end against your lower lip. Blow down hard on the paper. The free end of the paper will lift.

By blowing, you made the air on the upper surface of the paper move quickly. As the fast-flowing air moves away, it sucks the paper up. The slower-moving air on the lower surface pushes up, helping lift the paper.

Air tends to slide faster over the curved upper surface of a bird's wings. This air sucks the wings upward, while the slower-moving air under the wings pushes up. Flapping makes more air flow over a bird's wings.

This bluebird is coming in for a landing. See how it fans its wing feathers to slow itself down.

11

Besides giving a bird lift, its wings must move it forward. See the bump on the white ibis's chest? It is made by the two muscles that move the bird's wings. One muscle is really much bigger than the other. Its job is to pull the wings down. This is the power stroke of the wing beat. It makes air rush over the wing to lift the bird. It also moves the bird through the air. Muscles can only pull on bones, not push. So the second muscle loops over the bird's shoulder and attaches to the top of the wing bone. Its pull raises the wing to be ready for the next downstroke. Since the upstroke does not need to be as forceful, this muscle is much smaller.

Look closely at this white ibis's wing. The bones you can see look similar to the bones in your arm. Like your shoulder, elbow, and wrist joints, most birds' wings can bend in three places.

This eagle is hitching a ride on a thermal, a current of air that is warmed near the ground and then rises. The eagle's rather long and wide wings give it extra lift—enough to let it ride the air current without flapping at all.

If you watch, you'll see that bird wings are not all the same shape. Long, narrow wings, like those of albatrosses, are good for gliding. Such long wings let birds go long distances between wing flaps. Short, broad wings, like those of robins, are just right for birds that live in wooded areas. That wing shape gives a lot of lift for quick takeoffs and slow, steady flight between leafy tree branches.

Besides creating the wing's shape, flight feathers help in another way. During the upstroke, feathers at the wing's outer edge separate. Like opening a window blind, this lets the air slip through. And that makes it easier to pull the wing through the air. During the downstroke, these feathers are together and forced against the air. This helps to move the bird forward.

14

If you've ever watched a hummingbird, you know it can hover in one place. It can also fly straight up or backward. No other bird can match those flying tricks. Hummingbirds can fly this way because of their special wings.

Most birds, like the white ibis whose bones you could see, have three wing joints, which let the wing bend. Hummingbirds, though, have only one free-moving joint, so their wings are stiff. To see what this is like, fold your arm so your hand is as close to your shoulder as possible and wave your hand (not your fingers). A hummingbird can also tilt its wings the way you can turn your hand palm up and then palm down. This motion lets the hummingbird gain lift without moving forward.

This hummingbird's wings are flapping so fast they're a blur! Hummingbirds, the smallest birds, can flap their wings as much as 35 times a second. So you'll know just how fast that is, have someone count how many times you can wave your hand in one second.

By hovering, the hummingbird can reach tube-shaped flowers. Then it pokes in its long beak, sticks out its tongue, and laps up the flower's sugary liquid nectar.

Flying takes much energy, so birds eat energy-rich food, such as insects, worms, and seeds—and a lot of it. Some birds are thought of as pests because they eat food crops. Many others, though, are appreciated because they eat insect pests. Small adult birds will eat an amount of food equal to half their body weight in a day. Hummingbirds eat twice their weight in nectar. Imagine how much you would have to eat if you ate like a bird!

This waxwing parent swallowed the berries whole. When it reaches its nest, it coughs the fruit up for its babies. The parent will soon be off for more. While they're growing, the chicks may eat three times their weight in berries each day.

This hungry pelican chick is eating partly digested fish that the parent has coughed up for it.

Some birds, like the bluebird on page 11, carry food to their babies in their mouths. Others, like the waxwing and the pelican, swallow the food and carry it in a special sack called the crop. Then they cough up a meal for their young.

A bird's mouth is its beak. And each bird has a beak that's just the right shape for the food it eats.

The eagle uses its sharp beak in place of teeth to tear apart the meat it eats.

The cardinal's grooved upper beak holds onto the seed. The lower beak moves up, crushing the hard seed coat.

The frogmouth has a wide mouth with a short, flat beak— just right for catching insects.

A bird's feet are shaped to help it find food as well as to run, walk, scratch, and perch. See this purple gallinule's long yellow toes? They spread the bird's weight so it can walk easily across floating lily pads. As it walks, it hunts for insects and fish to eat.

Look at these bird toes tipped in sharp claws called talons. What would you guess this bird eats—seeds, nectar, or mice and other small animals? Did you guess that this bird is a hunter? This is an owl's foot. As the owl swoops down on a mouse, it swings its feet forward to catch its dinner.

Does it surprise you to learn that what look like legs are really this bird's feet? Like most birds, sandhill cranes walk on their toes. What look like knees bent the wrong way are really heels. What look like legs are really long feet.

A woodpecker has two toes pointed forward and two toes pointed backward to brace itself on a tree. Then it taps the trunk with its beak and listens. A hollow sound could mean an insect has made a tunnel in the wood. When it hears this, the woodpecker slams its beak over and over into the tree trunk. When it has made a hole, it pokes in its long tongue to catch the insect.

If you look at your tongue in the mirror, you'll see little bumps. These are covered with taste buds, which let you taste the food you eat. Woodpeckers and other birds have taste buds, too, but not nearly as many as you do. Since birds usually gulp down their food, there is little time to taste anything!

Woodpeckers have extra stiff, pointed tail feathers. They stick these against the tree for support while they drill for insects with their beaks.

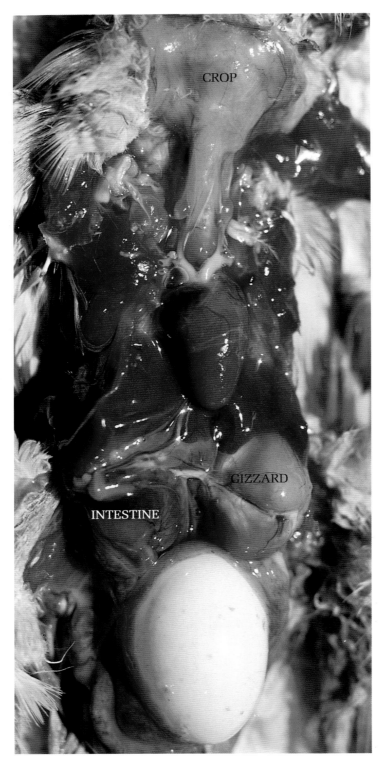

CROP

GIZZARD

INTESTINE

See the egg that was ready to be laid.

When the bird swallows, the food first goes into the crop. Food is stored in the crop until there's room in the bird's fore-stomach. Once in the fore-stomach, the food is mixed with special juices that start breaking it down. Next, muscles squeeze, pushing the food into the gizzard, where strong muscles do much the same job your teeth do when you chew your food. Some birds swallow sand or small stones to help the gizzard break down the food.

When the food has become a soft paste, muscles push it into the intestine. There still more juices break the food down into its basic building blocks, called *nutrients*. These move through the walls of the intestine into the blood. From there they travel through the bird's body, supplying it with the energy it needs to be active and to stay healthy.

Look at all the little stones inside this bird's gizzard. To keep the stones from cutting into the muscle, the gizzard has a tough lining.

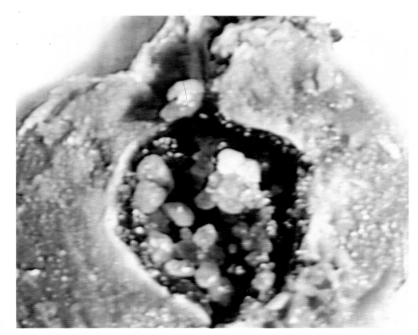

Not every part of what a bird eats can be broken down into a useful form. Carrying wastes also means carrying weight. So birds get rid of both liquid and solid wastes together in the form of thick white droppings.

Owls also have to get rid of another kind of waste. When they eat, owls swallow mice or other small animals whole. Owls' bodies can't break down fur, feathers, or bones, though. These parts remain in the stomach when the food moves on. There the wastes are packed together into a pellet that the owl coughs up. Do you see the mouse skull among the fur?

This robin parent is cleaning its nest. As soon as a baby bird is fed, it passes wastes in a soft sac. The parent quickly removes the sack before the nest or the baby gets wet.

Owl pellet

High-energy food and a lightweight body aren't all a bird needs. Its body also needs a steady supply of *oxygen*, one of the gases in the air. Oxygen combines with food nutrients to release the energy to be active and grow. A bird needs even more energy when it flies.

To get the oxygen it needs, a bird doesn't breathe the way you do. When you breathe in, air flows through tubes into tiny bubble-like sacs in the lungs where oxygen is exchanged for the waste gas *carbon dioxide.* Then you breathe this waste gas out before breathing in more oxygen. When a bird breathes in, most of the air bypasses the lungs and goes into special balloon-like sacs, where it is stored. When the bird breathes out, this stored air moves into the lungs. There it passes through millions of tiny tubes, sort of like water flowing through a sponge. Oxygen is exchanged for carbon dioxide. As the bird breathes in again, the air in the lungs moves into more holding sacs, where it is stored until the bird breathes out the next time. Then the air leaves the bird's body.

This male prairie chicken is all puffed up to attract a mate. What look like yellow balloons are really patches of skin stretched by this bird's special balloon-like air storage sacs.

HEART

To meet its great need for oxygen and food nutrients, a bird has a big heart for its body size.

The bird's blood carries oxygen and nutrients throughout its body. And the pump that pushes the blood around a bird's body is its heart. It lies below the lungs inside the chest. The heart is a muscle. But a bird does not control its heartbeat the way it does its wing flaps. The heart has a built-in pacemaker that sets it beating. And the bird's brain controls how fast or slow the heart pumps.

See the clear eyelids partly covering this owl's eyes? All birds have these extra eyelids. They slip across quickly, like a windshield wiper, keeping the eyes clean and moist.

This is the layer called the retina at the back of a bird's eyes. What looks like a ridge is called the pecten. Your eyes don't have a pecten. No one is quite sure what it does for birds. Some experts think it helps a bird spot movement that could mean danger is nearby. Others think it helps supply the eyes with blood carrying oxygen and nutrients to keep them healthy.

Sight is usually a bird's best sense. Light passes through a hole in the eye—the pupil—that looks like a black spot. It also passes through the lens and the crystal-clear jelly inside the eye. At the back of the eye, the light strikes the *retina*. The retina is made up of special light-sensitive cells. Signals from these cells are sent to the brain. The brain figures out those messages, and the bird sees. This all happens almost instantly.

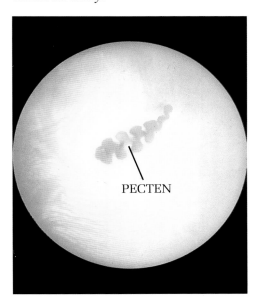

PECTEN

Can you spot the owl's ears? Don't try too hard! Birds' ears are usually hidden by feathers. Sounds are really invisible waves of air that easily get through the feathers. Then the waves pass through a short canal, bump into the eardrum, and set the bones of the middle ear in motion. Finally, the sound waves reach the inner ear, where there are special cells that send messages to the brain. Like the signals sent from the eye, the brain figures these out. Then the bird hears.

Many birds can also make sounds. They have a special song box, called a *syrinx*, in their chests. Air passes from the lungs through the syrinx on its way out the throat. Muscles squeeze the syrinx to make its opening change shape. Then air escaping through the opening makes a sound.

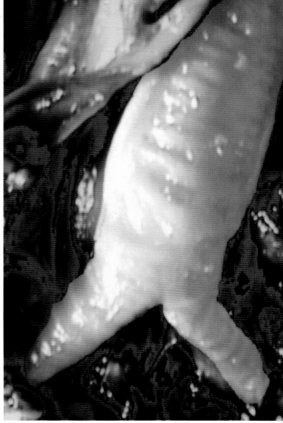

COMPUTER COLOR-ENHANCED

This is a pigeon's song box, or syrinx. The single tube is the bird's windpipe. The two branches go to the bird's lungs.

Because owls often hunt in the dark, hearing is especially important to them. This bird's disk-shaped face helps direct sounds into its ears. One ear is also higher than the other, so sounds reach the ears at slightly different times. This helps the owl judge where the sound is coming from.

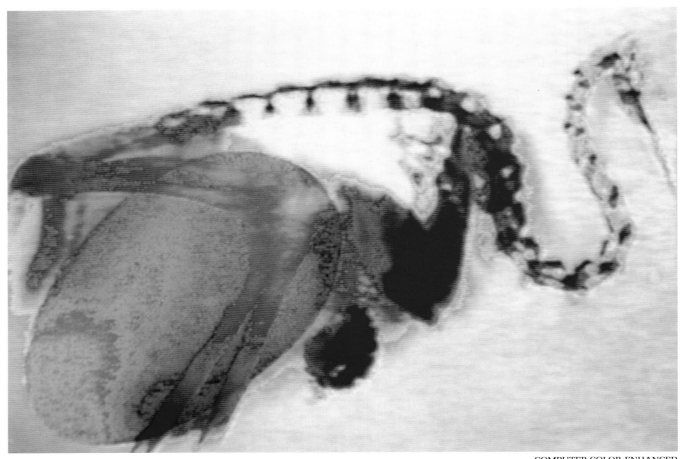

COMPUTER COLOR-ENHANCED

This X ray lets you peek inside the female kiwi's body. See the big egg ready to be laid? This bird, which is about the size of a chicken, lays an unusually large egg for its size. The egg is about twelve centimeters (five inches) long and weighs about 450 grams (one pound). To get an idea of how this compares, hold a pound of butter in one hand and a chicken's egg in the other.

If you crack open a chicken egg, you'll see the yellow *yolk* inside. Although the whole thing—white and yolk and shell—is called an egg, the yolk is the real egg. It forms inside the mother's body and moves through a tube, where it is wrapped in the *albumen*, or egg white. As the egg nears the end of the tube, it is coated with minerals that harden into the shell. If a father bird mates with the mother, a sperm will join the egg before it is wrapped and coated. Then something very special happens. The upper part of the yolk changes, growing into a chick. The food needed for this growth is supplied by the rest of the yolk.

This mother grebe is just laying an egg. Look closely and you'll see the egg coming out of her body.

The baby coot's feathers are wet when it hatches. They will soon dry and become fluffy.

EGG TOOTH

After their eggs are laid, most birds sit on them to keep them warm. Sometimes only one parent does this job, but often both take turns. Inside its eggshell, the baby bird grows until it is ready to hatch. That usually takes only a few weeks.

It's no wonder this baby coot looks tired. It just finished the hard job of pecking open its shell. See the tiny bump on its beak? That is the egg tooth the chick used to chip a hole in the eggshell. The egg tooth will drop off in a few days.

With only a coat of downy feathers, a chick could be quickly chilled by cold water. So this baby black-necked swan is given a ride while its parent hunts for food.

In only a few weeks, the young swan will grow its adult feathers. Then it will be able to take care of itself. Best of all, the young bird will be able to spread its wings and—with a little practice—fly. Clearly birds are special...from the inside out!

THINGS TO DO

Now that you know something about birds, go outdoors. When you see or hear a bird, be still, look, and listen. What is the bird doing? Is it alone or with other birds? If it's flying, is it flapping or gliding? If the bird's eating, try to see what it is eating. If the bird's singing, try to copy its song. Can you get the bird to answer you?

Instead of going in search of birds, you could invite them to come near your house or apartment. Here are a couple of easy ways to make hungry birds feel welcome.

*String popcorn and drape the strings over bushes or a balcony railing.

*Tie a string around the bigger end of a pinecone. Mix peanut butter with cornmeal or oatmeal and press onto the cone. Roll in birdseed and hang outside.

Or you and your family could plant bushes, trees, and flowers in your yard to attract birds. Any tubular flower, such as coral honeysuckle and fuchsia, are favorites with hummingbirds. Cherry trees, raspberries, and blueberries will draw cardinals, waxwings, bluebirds, and other birds in summer. Hollies will attract many birds in winter, including waxwings and thrashers. To find out more ways to attract birds, write the National Wildlife Federation, 1400 Sixteenth Street NW, Washington, DC 20036-2266, and request the Backyard Wildlife Habitat Information Packet (item 79919).

If you live in a city, you'll probably find lots of pigeons as close as your nearest park. Watch one of these birds walk and then try to mimic it. Did you remember to bob your head like a pigeon? What different colors are the pigeons? If you'd like to watch the pigeons eat, take along stale bread torn into small pieces or shelled peanuts to toss out. How do the birds react? Are they good at sharing?

If you'd like to see for yourself what an owl's been eating, you could check out an owl pellet like the one on page 24. Owl pellets are clean and dry and don't smell. You can order single owl pellets from scientific supply companies. One source is Carolina Biological Supply Company, 2700 York Road, Burlington, North Carolina 27215 (phone: 800-334-5551). Ask for catalog item P1680. Owl pellets are also available from The Carolina Raptor Center, P.O. Box 16443, Charlotte, North Carolina 28297 (phone: 704-875-6521).

PRONUNCIATION GUIDE

ALBUMEN	al-byü'-mən
CARBON DIOXIDE	kär'-bən dī-äk'-sīd,
CONTOUR	kän'-tu̇r,
MUSCLES	mə'-səls
NUTRIENTS	nü'-trē-ənts
OXYGEN	äk'-si-jən
RETINA	re'-tᵊn-ə
SKELETON	ske'-lə-tᵊn
SYRINX	sir'-iŋ(k)s
TALONS	ta'-ləns
YOLK	yōk'

ä as in cart	ə as in banana	ŋ as in sing
u̇ as in pull	ü as in rule	

GLOSSARY/INDEX

AIR SACS: Balloon-like sacs that hold air before and after it passes through the lungs. **25**

BEAK: Body part used to get food. The shape is suited to what the bird eats. For example, finches have short, heavy beaks to crack seeds. **6, 7, 9, 17–18, 21**

BONES: The hard but lightweight parts that form the body's supporting frame. Many bones are nearly hollow and are filled with balloon-like air sacs. Their lightness helps make it possible for flying birds to get airborne. **8–9, 12, 13, 24**

BRAIN: Body part that receives messages about what is happening inside and outside the body. The brain sends messages to put the body into action. **26–27**

CARBON DIOXIDE: Gas that is naturally given off in body activities, carried to the lungs by the blood, and breathed out. **25**

CHICKS: The name given to baby birds. Some, like ducks, are well developed when they hatch, have feathers, and are quickly able to feed themselves. Others, like robins, are naked, have their eyes closed, and are helpless when they hatch. **16–17, 24, 31–33**

CROP: A body part where food is usually stored for a short time. **22–23**

EGG: Although the white, yolk, and shell are called the egg, the yolk is the real egg. The yolk is produced by the mother bird's body. When joined by a special cell, the sperm, from a father bird, the upper part of the yolk changes, growing into a chick. The rest of the yolk supplies food for the chick until it has developed enough to hatch. **30–32**

FEATHERS: Unique to birds, these are outgrowths of special cells in the skin. Feathers are a bird's main protective covering. In birds that fly, tiny hooks "zip" wing feathers together for an airtight surface. Some male birds have brightly colored or decorative feathers to attract a mate. **4, 5, 6, 21, 24, 32, 33**

FEET: Body parts that support the bird when it stands or perches. Like its beak, a bird's feet are suited to how it lives. For example, a cardinal's feet have three toes in front and one behind to help it grip a branch. A pelican's feet have webbing or skin stretched between the toes to help it swim. **6, 19–20**

FORE-STOMACH: Usually a bird's stomach has two parts—the fore-stomach, where special juices help break down the food, and the gizzard, which grinds the partly digested food into a soft paste. **22–23**

GIZZARD: This muscular body part helps birds break down the food they eat. Birds often swallow sand, pebbles, fruit pits, or other hard bits which collect in the gizzard and help it grind up the food. Most of the grit stays in the gizzard, but some is passed out with wastes and has to be replaced. **22–23**

HEART: Body part that acts like a pump, constantly pushing blood throughout the bird's body. **26**

INTESTINE: The long, winding tube where food is mixed with special juices to break it down into nutrients. These nutrients then pass into the blood and are carried throughout the bird's body. **22–23**

LUNGS: Body part where oxygen and carbon dioxide are exchanged inside tiny tubes. **25**

MUSCLES: Working in pairs, these move the bird's bones by pulling on them. Largest are the breast muscles that power the wing's downstroke. **9, 12, 23**

NECTAR: Sweet, energy-rich liquid produced in flowers to attract birds, insects, and animals. **16**

NUTRIENTS: Chemical building blocks into which food is broken down for use by the bird's body. The five basic nutrients provided by foods are proteins, fats, carbohydrates, minerals, and vitamins. **23, 26**

OXYGEN: A gas in the air that is breathed into the lungs and passed to the blood. Then the blood carries it throughout the body. Oxygen is combined with food nutrients to release energy. **25–26**

PECTEN: A ridge on the retina of a bird's eye. While no one is sure what it does, some experts think it helps a bird sense movement. Others think it provides the eye with an additional blood supply. **27**

PREEN GLAND: Body part that some birds have to produce an oil that's collected with the beak and spread on the feathers. This coating helps keep the feathers from breaking. **7**

PREENING: Steps a bird goes through to care for its feathers. Many birds use their beaks to remove dirt and "zip up" any of the little hooks holding the feathers together that may have come apart. **6, 7**

RETINA: Layer at the back of the eye which is made up of light-sensitive cells. When light strikes the cells, messages are sent to the brain. The brain figures out these messages, and the birds sees. **27**

SYRINX: The song box that produces sound when air escaping from the lungs moves two stretched bands. **29**

WINGS: Body part needed for flight. A bird's wings have a special shape that is just right for its style of flying. For example, long, slim wings help seabirds soar in strong winds. Short, stubby wings make it easy for partridges to fly among forest trees. **10–15**

PHOTO CREDITS

Cover Isidor Jeklin
p. 1   Cornell Laboratory of Ornithology
p. 2   The Atlanta Zoo
p. 3   Jeff Foott
p. 4   The Zoological Society of San Diego
p. 5   Bruce J. Russell, Biomedia Associates
p. 6   Billie Reaney, computer color-enhanced by Steve Mann
p. 7   Jeff Foott
p. 8   Willard J. Gould DVM; Dr. James E. McIntosh and Mr. Robert Spears,
       Department of Biomedical Sciences, Baylor College of Dentistry, Dallas, Texas
p. 9   Doug Wechsler/VIREO
p. 10 Cornell Laboratory of Ornithology
p. 11 Isidor Jeklin
p. 13 Cornell Laboratory of Ornithology
p. 14 Cornell Laboratory of Ornithology
p. 15 Rob Curtis
p. 16 Cornell Laboratory of Ornithology
p. 17 Cornell Laboratory of Ornithology
p. 18 Texas Parks and Wildlife; Steve and Dave Maslowski; C. Volpe/VIREO
p. 19 Cornell Laboratory of Ornithology
p. 20 Cornell Laboratory of Ornithology (both)
p. 21 Cornell Laboratory of Ornithology
p. 22 Willard J. Gould DVM
p. 23 Steve Mann
p. 24 Cornell Laboratory of Ornithology (both)
p. 25 Cornell Laboratory of Ornithology
p. 26 Willard J. Gould DVM
p. 27 Natural Elements Photo-Research, Inc./Greg R. Homel; Willard J. Gould DVM
p. 28 Steve and Dave Maslowski
p. 29 Steve Mann
p. 30 Otorohanga Zoological Society, computer color-enhanced by Steve Mann
p. 31 Keith A. Szafranski
p. 32 Natural Elements Photo-Research, Inc./Greg R. Homel
p. 33 The Zoological Society of San Diego
p. 36 Texas Parks and Wildlife